THAT'S NO *ORDINARY* ZAMBONI! LOOK--IT... IT'S...

AND WOULDN'T YOU KNOW WHO'S PERCHED UP AT THE *HEAD*...

（22）

FROM THE CORNER, NOSEDIVE SHOOTS IT ACROSS THE ICE--

MALLORY DRIVES THE PUCK LEFT, PULLING THE GOALIE AROUND--

SHE SNAP-PASSES IT TO DUKE, WHO HAD FAKED OUT THE DEFENDERS-- HE SHOOTS--HE SCORES!

:SNORT: BAH!

BOUND BY THE I.G.H.* RULES HE'S BEEN ESPOUSING, LORD DRAGAUNUS RELUCTANTLY POSTS THE DUCKS' SCORE.

01 01

* INTERGALACTIC HOCKEY.

AND SO, THE STAGE IS SET FOR THE MOST COSMIC, AWE-INSPIRING HOCKEY BATTLE EVER CONCEIVED...

YOU'RE GOIN' DOWN, DUCKLING! WOTTAYA SAY TO THAT?

I SKATE, THEREFORE I AM!

SO *THAT'S* HOW IT CAME ABOUT. IMAGINE MY SURPRISE, WHEN YOU ALL CAME TO *FETCH* ME!

YES. AND IMAGINE *OUR* SURPRISE WHEN WE SAW...*YOU*.

I HAVE *WONDERED* WHAT IT WOULD BE LIKE, TO BE A *SOLDIER*.

I HAVE A HUNCH I MAY DO *MORE* THAN JUST "*OBSERVE*"!

THE TROOP RETURNS FOR ORDERS, TO HEADQUARTERS CAMP.

THERE PHOEBUS IS ABSORBED IN STRATEGY WITH THE FRENCH KING'S EMISSARY...

HIS MAJESTY'S *ENEMIES* ARE AMASSING IN FULL FORCE! WE MUST BE PREPARED, HERE...AND HERE... AND *HERE*...

Mm. Yes. Hm.

AND TO *FURTHER* BEDEVIL US, THE INFAMOUS *BLACK PATROL* IS RUMORED TO HAVE BEEN SIGHTED, NEAR *CONFLICT RIDGE*...

 # PEGASUS CLOUD MAZE

STORMY SKIES THREATEN TO KEEP
PEGASUS FROM FINDING HIS WAY
HOME... USE YOUR HORSE SENSE AND
HELP HIM LOCATE HERCULES!

ALL RIGHT! IT'S TIME TO BE A *REAL DINOSAUR!*

HERE I COME, WOOD*EEEEEEE!*

sproing!

Wha-hoo!

SCATTER, MEN! *INCOMING REPTILE!*

CRASH!

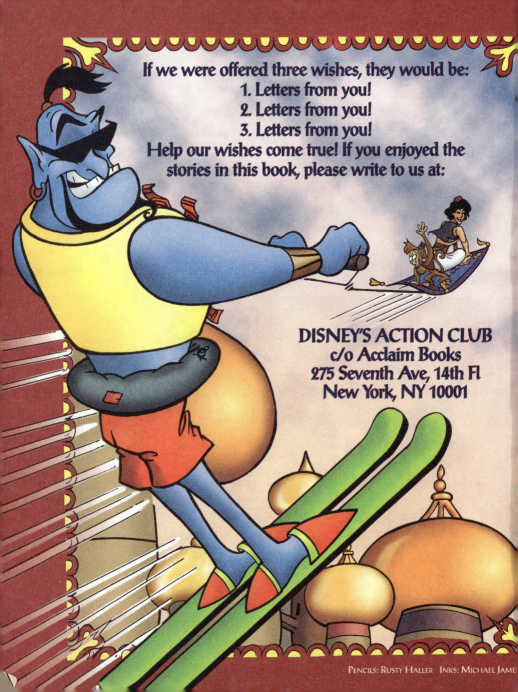

If we were offered three wishes, they would be:
1. Letters from you!
2. Letters from you!
3. Letters from you!
Help our wishes come true! If you enjoyed the stories in this book, please write to us at:

DISNEY'S ACTION CLUB
c/o Acclaim Books
275 Seventh Ave, 14th Fl
New York, NY 10001

PENCILS: RUSTY HALLER INKS: MICHAEL JAME